Mix and Max
Take Off

Marion Kemp and Sheila Lane

Illustrated by Andy Cooke

Series editor **Penni Cotton**
Senior Lecturer, Reading and Language Studies
Kingston Polytechnic

To Parents

By sharing books together at home you can play a vital part in helping your child learn to read.

The books at Level 3 in this series are for children who are progressing towards reading fluently on their own. The play format gives the support necessary for children to enjoy reading with you and yet lets them read their own part and thus gain confidence as independent readers.

How to read this book together

▷ Make reading together a comfortable and special time.

▷ **The role of Max is for you to read and your child reads Mix**. Explain that you don't read out the speaker's name each time, it is just there to help tell you when it's your turn.

▷ Introduce the story slowly by looking at page 5 and talking about the characters. Perhaps your child is already familiar with them from other books in the *Parent and Child Programme*.

Help your child, particularly on the first reading, by giving the difficult words so you don't slow up the pace of the story or by reading both parts initially.

Encourage your child to use the pictures to guess or predict what is happening.

If your child is stuck just give the word yourself. This is far more helpful than sounding out individual letters.

Always praise good guesses — much of the skill in reading is in guessing or predicting what the word will be.

Your child will probably enjoy reading the story with you again and again — this is valuable in building confidence and practising reading.

Always end reading together on a positive note.

Max I've had a really good idea, Mix.
I've nearly finished tying
these balloons.

5

Max   Come and look, Mix!
What do you think of my new
invention?

Mix   What is it?

Max   It's a balloon bus.
How would you like to go for a ride
up in the sky?

6

Mix No thanks!

Max Well, come and sit inside for a
minute. It can't take off you know.

Mix How do I know?

Max Because I've weighted it down with
a stone.

Mix It's a bit small for two.

Max Come on, try it! Get in with me.

7

Max   Well! How do you like it?

Mix   Not much!

Max   I suppose it is rather a squash.
I know! There's a bigger pot in the
shed. What about using that?

Mix   Good idea!

Max   This is better. Now what shall I call it? How about Max?

Mix   Or Mix?

Max   I'm the one who invented it.

Mix   Call it Max then.

Max   I know! We could call it Maxibus.

Mix   Yes! Maxibus, I like that.

Max   Shall we go for a ride? We can take some food. How about a packet of cheese nibbles?

Mix   I'll take a box of cheese.

Max   Do we need anything else?

Mix   Apples! I like red ones.

Max   What about some chocolate bars?

Mix   Yes, good idea!

10

Max Are we ready now?

Mix I think so.

Max It's just the day to launch the Maxibus. Come on! Get in!

Mix I'm in!

Max Ready for countdown? You count
and I'll throw the stone out on ZERO.

Mix Ten

Nine

Eight

Seven

Six

Five

Four

Three

Two

One

Mix
+ Max ZERO!

Max   We're off!
Up we go,
ho, ho, ho!
Flying high . . .

Mix   . . . in the sky!

Max   What about that!
We've made a rhyme.

Mix   I'm the one who made it.

Max   Let's say it again.

Mix + Max   Up we go,
ho, ho, ho!
Flying high
in the sky!

Max   Mix! Look down there!

Mix   I can see Cruncher.
Cruncher! Cruncher!
Look at us!

Max   He's going for a swim in the river.

Mix   I'll drop an apple by him.
Plop!

Max   He's looking up! He thinks it's
raining apples!

Mix   Is that Sally Cat by the tree?

Max   That's her! I wonder if she's seen us up here?

Mix   She has! Look at her face!

Max   Let's call down to her. Silly old Sally!

Mix + Max   Silly old Sally!

Mix   You can't get us now!

Max   Look! There's a huge bird in that tree.

Mix   Oh, Max! It's an owl.

Max   Then we're heading for trouble. Owls eat mice, you know.

Mix   I think she's asleep.

16

Max   Let's try to fly away before she wakes up. Quick! Pull at the strings on this side. Come on! Pull!

Mix   I am pulling!

Max   She's opening one eye.
Come on, Mix! Pull harder!

Mix   Don't fall out, Max!
Don't fall out!

Max   It's all right.
She can't see us now.

17

Max Phew! We'd have made a tasty snack for that owl.

Mix Oooh! Did you say snack? Let's have some cheese.

Max Would you like Gorgonzola, Cheddar or Brie?

Mix Cheddar, please.

Max   Mix, would you like to go down now?

Mix   No! I like it up here.

Max   But it's getting windy and we're tossing about. I'm beginning to feel . . . a bit . . . air sick.

Mix   You've had too much cheese.

Max   Yuk! Don't talk to me about cheese, please.

19

Mix   Wow! This is fun!
I do like it up here.

Max   I don't! I feel terrible.
I feel ill, really ill.

Mix   I told you! You had
too much cheese.

Max   Please! Don't mention cheese!

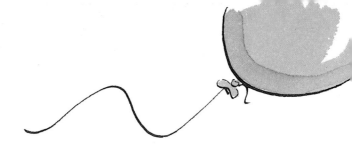

Mix   Max! Max!
Look up there!

Max   Oh no! It's one of our balloons. It
must have broken loose in the wind.

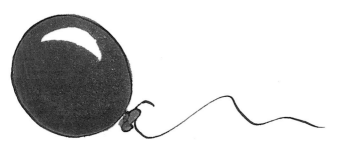

Mix   Look! There's another
one.

Max   Never mind! The rest are OK.

Mix   We're going down a bit.

Max   That's good! I feel better now.

21

Mix Look over there in the sky, Max. What is it?

Max I think it's a sea-gull.
Yes, it is! Maybe she's coming to see if we've got any food.

Mix I'll give her some cheese.

Max Good idea! You can give her all the cheese if you like.

Mix This is fun!

Max There's another one coming now.

Mix I'll give him some cheese too.

Max I'm not sure you should feed them, Mix.

Mix   Well, they are a bit big.

Max   Look out, Mix! Don't give them any more cheese. They're pecking the balloons.

Mix   Shoo! Shoo!
Go away! Go away!

Max   We mustn't let them land on our Maxibus.

Mix + **Max**   Shoo! SHOO!

24

Mix   Max! Look over there!

Max   Oh, no! A whole flock of them.
Now we're in trouble.

Mix   What shall we do?

Max   Drive them away or we'll fall.

25

Mix   Shoo! Shoo!
Go away! G O A W A Y !

Max   Help! That one has got the pot in
its claws. We're tipping over . . .

Mix   Hold on to me, Max!

Max   Mix! Mix!
I'm frightened!

Mix   We're going down!

Mix
+ Max   HELP!

27

Max　We're going to drown.
I know we're going to drown . . . !

Mix　No, we're not! Look!
Here's our pot. Hold on
to me.

Max　Help me in! Help me in! Help!

Mix　It's all right, Max!
You're in!

Max　We must get to dry land.
Paddle, Mix! Paddle over to
that island.

Mix   Look! It's not an island.
It's Cruncher!

Max   Hurray! It's our friend Cruncher.
We're safe.

Mix   What a day!

Max   And we did fly high
in the sky!